THE VERY
HUNGRY
BEAR

NICK BLAND

Tor
Mexi

For Andrew McMillan.

Scholastic Canada Ltd.
604 King Street West, Toronto, Ontario M5V 1E1, Canada

Scholastic Inc.
557 Broadway, New York, NY 10012, USA

Scholastic Australia Pty Limited
PO Box 579, Gosford, NSW 2250, Australia

Scholastic New Zealand Limited
Private Bag 94407, Botany, Manukau 2163, New Zealand

Scholastic Children's Books
Euston House, 24 Eversholt Street, London NW1 1DB, UK

www.scholastic.ca

Library and Archives Canada Cataloguing in Publication

Bland, Nick, 1973-, author, illustrator
The very hungry bear / Nick Bland.

Previously published: 2012.
ISBN 978-1-4431-6312-5 (softcover)

I. Title.

PZ10.3.B527Veh 2018   j823'.92   C2017-904027-8

5 4 3 2 1   Printed in China 38   18 19 20 21 22

Bear was in a **GRUMPY** mood,
he hadn't eaten any food,
and he couldn't catch a single fish to cook.

He'd been hungry since the break of day
and every fish had got away . . .

Now suddenly something huge
was on his hook.

(YANK!)

He cranked the handle round and round.
He yanked the line and wound and wound.
He flicked it here . . . and waved it over there.

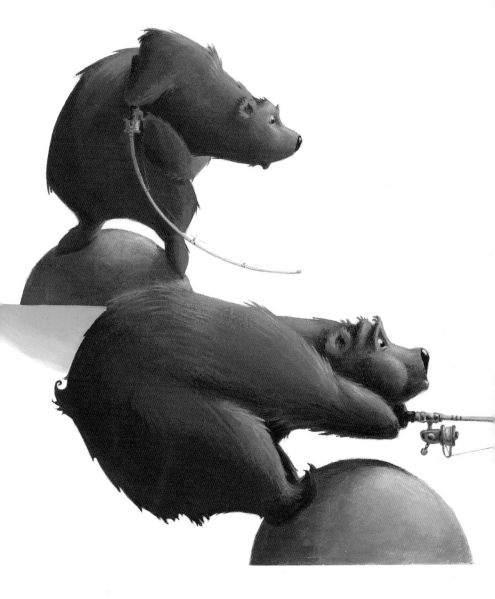

A hungry bear is very strong,
so it didn't take him very long
to discover that he'd caught . . .

A POLAR BEAR!

"Excuse me," said Bear.
"Do you have to fish there?
You are catching all of the fish."

"I'm sorry," he said,
as he lifted his head.
"You can have one of mine if you wish."

Then he added with a smile,
"You can have the whole pile,
if you'll just find me somewhere to stay.

My iceberg is shrinking
and soon I'll be sinking
and my home's such a long way away."

Now a fish to a bear
is like a chocolate éclair,
it's incredibly hard to resist.

So the thought of a pile
that would last for a while
was an offer too good to be missed!

With a splosh and a splish
and an armful of fish,
Bear led the way through the trees.

"My cave's over there
and I'm happy to share.
You can stay for as long as you please."

But his guest shook his head,
"I'm so sorry," he said.
"While your cave is particularly nice,
it's just a bit hot
for this coat that I've got
and the fire is melting my ice."

So they went to see Mole,
and he dug them a hole,
which was cooler . . . but just a bit small.

And they visited Croc,
on his cool river rock.
But he wasn't that helpful at all.

"Perhaps this is best!"
said the bear, from a nest.

"But I think that I'm
going to sneeze!"

Then he squinted his eyes
and he said, with surprise,
"Ahhh . . .

I'm allergic to trees."

So the bear with white hair
followed right behind Bear
to the only place left they could go.
Away from the trees
and the warm summer breeze . . .

All the way **UP** to the snow.

They built him a home
with an icy-white dome,

and Bear left a house-warming dish.

With a smile and a wave
Bear went back to his cave . . .

And he stopped on the way for a fish.